HODDER CHILDREN'S BOOKS
First published in Great Britain in 2017 by Hodder and Stoughton

A CIP catalogue record for this book is available from the British Library.

PB ISBN: 978 1 444 92725 2
HB ISBN: 978 1 444 92724 5

10 9 8 7 6 5 4 3 2 1

For Lucy - P.B.
For Aria - S.M.

Printed and bound in China

MIX
Paper from
responsible sources
FSC® C104740

Hodder Children's Books
An imprint of Hachette Children's Group
Part of Hodder and Stoughton
Carmelite House
50 Victoria Embankment
London EC4Y 0DZ

An Hachette UK Company
www.hachette.co.uk
www.hachettechildrens.co.uk

A Recipe for Playtime

Peter Bently
& Sarah Massini

Hodder
Children's
Books

Baby, baby, bright as day,
Up and dressed and off to play!

Hurry, hurry, come with me
And hear my playtime recipe.

Take a box of coloured blocks.
Lift up lid. Tip up box.

See them rising...
add one more...

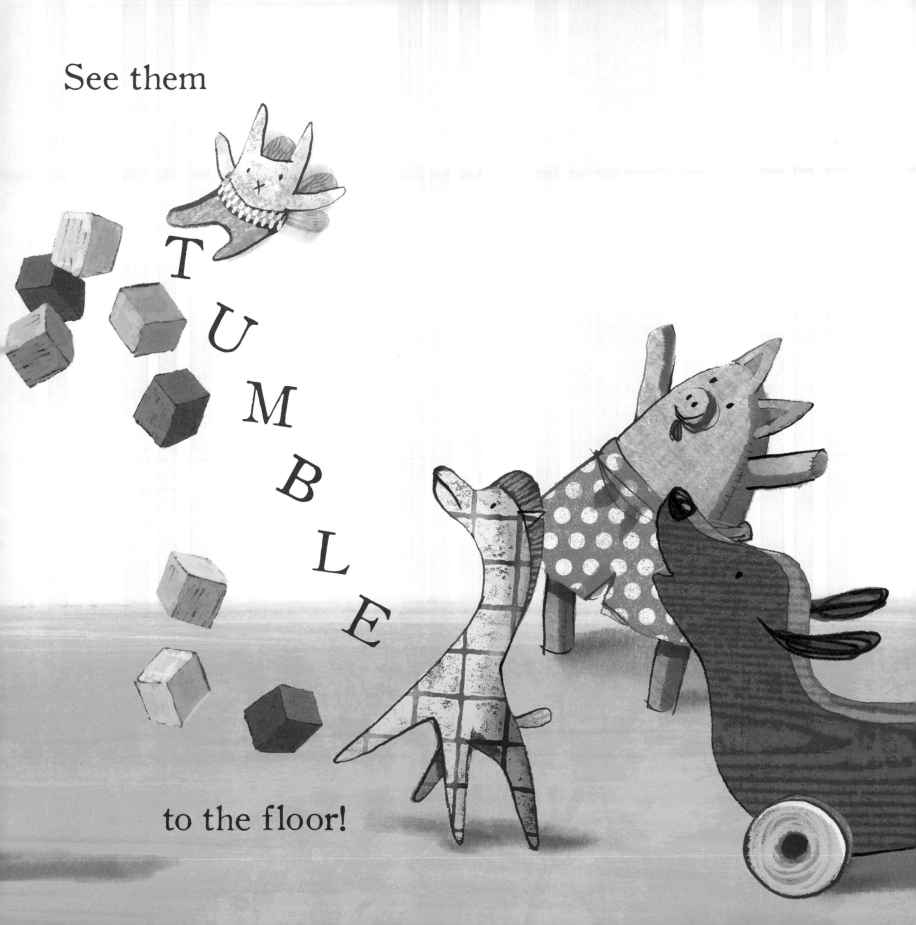

See them

T
U
M
B
L
E

to the floor!

Take a pot of paint or two.

Yellow,

red,

a splash of blue.

Clean up table. Leave to dry.
Whisk up baby. See him fly!

Heap up cushions. Make a train.

Toot toot CRASH!

'Again, again!'

Pick up baby. Place on saddle.

Giddy up and off to battle!

Wrap up baby.
Take outside.

Up the steps –

and down the slide!

Swing down low. Now swing up HIGH!

Next it's time for hide-and-seek.
Count to twenty. Mustn't peek!

Coming baby, ready or not!

Getting warmer...

9
10
12
8
11
13
7
14
6
15
5
4
16
17
3
18
2
19
1
20

warmer... HOT!

Head indoors to play at chase.
Speedy baby wins the race!

Add a trumpet and a drum!
Root-i-toot and tum-ti-tum!

Play a merry marching song.
Put things back where they belong.

When all is tidy, take a book.
Find a cosy little nook.

Snuggle baby on a lap.

Cover baby. Leave to nap.

Softly,
softly,
creep away.

Soon we'll all be back to play.